BMX CHALLENGE

SPORT STORIES

TEXT BY

THOMAS K.

ILLUSTRATIONS BY

IFFANY

D1630774

Raintree is an imprint of Capstone Global Library Limited, a company incorporated in England and Wales having its registered office at 264 Banbury Road, Oxford, OX2 7DY – Registered company number: 6695582

www.raintree.co.uk
myorders@raintree.co.uk

Text © Capstone Global Library Limited 2018
The moral rights of the proprietor have been asserted.

Designed by Russell Griesmer
Original illustrations © Capstone Global Library Limited 2018
Illustrated by Sean Tiffany
Production by Tori Abraham
Originated by Capstone Global Library Limited
Printed and bound in China

ISBN 978 1 4747 3232 1
21 20 19 18 17
10 9 8 7 6 5 4 3 2 1

British Library Cataloguing in Publication Data
A full catalogue record for this book is available from the British Library.

CONTENTS

CHAPTER 1

BIG MOUTH

At the bikerack behind Johnson Middle School, Jason Tillman unlocked his bike. He looked up and saw three boys from the year above. They hopped onto their bikes and pulled on their helmets. Wearing their funny helmets, they reminded Jason of astronauts.

"Nice helmets, guys," Jason called. As soon as he said it, he wished he hadn't. But it was too late. The words were out.

"What'd you say?" asked Paul, the biggest boy in the group. He stuck his helmet under his arm and walked over to Jason.

"Nothing," Jason said. "You just look like you're going to blast off for the moon any second." Jason smiled to show he was kidding. To his surprise, Paul smiled back.

"This is what BMX bikers wear," Paul said. He stuck the helmet onto his head. "You know, pro riders who can handle the dirt and like catching some air."

"BMX biking?" Jason repeated. He shook his head. "That's nothing big. Little kids can do that stuff."

The boys behind Paul laughed. Paul shook his head. "If it's so easy," he said, "let's see you do it."

Uh-oh, Jason thought. *Now I've done it. Me and my big mouth.* He had no idea how to ride a BMX bike.

"I would," Jason said, "but I don't have a little bike like you guys. I just have my mountain bike. Sorry."

Jason put his foot on the pedal of his bike, ready to take off.

"Sounds like you're just scared," Paul muttered. "Are you scared to try something a little child could do?"

Jason turned and said, "I'm not scared. I just can't do BMX stuff with my big-boy bike. I'd need a baby bike like yours."

"Meet us behind the Pine Grove Shopping Centre tonight," Paul said. "I have an extra 'baby' bike you can ride. I'll even bring a space helmet for you."

Jason frowned. "I don't know," he said. "It's probably not –"

"I dare you to be there, Jason," Paul said, interrupting him. "Are you going to wimp out?"

Jason was silent. How was he supposed to back down from a dare? He didn't want to look like a baby. "Fine, I'll be there," he muttered.

Paul smirked and rode off with his friends. They laughed as they left Jason standing alone in the car park.

CHAPTER 2

THE DARE

"Jason!" a voice yelled across the school car park. Jason was so startled he almost fell off his bike. It was his best friend, Stephen Harris.

"Thanks for waiting for me," Stephen said. He held up a textbook. "I almost forgot my book. Tomorrow's maths test would be pretty hard without this."

Stephen unlocked his bike. "What's the matter with you?" he asked. "You look freaked out."

"I am," Jason replied. "You know Paul Hansen, that tall boy in the year above?"

Stephen nodded. Jason told his friend what had happened. "So he dared you?" Stephen asked when Jason had finished.

"Yeah," Jason replied. "And you know my rule about dares." Jason never backed down from a dare. Ever.

"I know," Stephen said. "That stupid rule is always getting you into trouble."

Stephen was right. Jason had a bad history with dares. He'd sprained his ankle last year when a neighbour dared him to jump off the roof. And last term he'd ended up with detention for a month after someone dared him to start a food fight in the canteen.

Stephen and Jason rode out of the Johnson Middle School car park and onto the street.

"You should just forget about it," Stephen said once they were further down the road.

"I can't," Jason said. "A dare is a dare. I can't let them think I'm a chicken."

"You have to learn to keep your mouth shut," Stephen said. "I told you!"

"I know, I know," Jason said. "Sometimes I can't help it, though. The words just come out and get me into trouble."

Stephen hopped over a pothole in the road and slowed to a stop at the street corner. He balanced for a moment, squeezing the brakes a few times. Jason stopped next to him.

"Can you come with me?" Jason asked.

"What?" Stephen asked. "You're not actually going to meet them, are you?"

"I have to at least try," Jason said.

"That's crazy," Stephen said. "You don't know anything about BMX bikes. My brother, David, used to ride, but even he hasn't ridden since –"

"That's perfect," Jason interrupted. "You can teach me some of the tricks David used to do! You can be my coach!"

Stephen groaned. "Talking about tricks won't help you, Jason!" he said. "You have to practise to be good at that stuff."

"Please?" Jason asked. He put his hands together. "Don't make your best friend beg, because I'll do it. I'll kneel down right here on the ground."

"You wouldn't," Stephen said.

"Want to dare me?" Jason asked. He started to climb off of his bike.

"No!" Stephen cried. "You and these stupid dares! That's what got you into trouble in the first place!"

Jason smiled. He knew he could count on Stephen. He just knew it.

CHAPTER 3

HIDDEN TRACK

That night at dinner, all Jason could think about was the BMX dare.

"Is everything all right, Jason?" his mother asked. "You're awfully quiet tonight."

"I'm fine," Jason mumbled. "I'm just not hungry."

Maybe Stephen's right, Jason thought. *Maybe I should just forget the dare.*

He was about to grab the phone to call Stephen. Just then, there was a knock at the front door.

Jason's little sister, Tina, raced for the door. "Hey, Jason," she shouted a moment later. "Stevie's here!"

When Jason got to the doorway, Stephen was waiting. "Are you ready for the bike ride?" he asked with a sigh.

* * *

Jason and Stephen rode through town until they reached the shopping centre. Behind the shops, a BMX track stood in a clearing among a cluster of trees.

Jason could see Paul and his friends through the trees. They were riding their bikes on a dirt track that twisted back and forth.

"I never knew there was a dirt track back there," Stephen whispered.

"Neither did I," Jason admitted.

"Dave thinks you're crazy, by the way," Stephen said. "He says you can get hurt if you're not careful."

"He's probably right," Jason said. "Let's get out of here before they see us."

"Hey, Tillman!" Paul suddenly shouted.

Paul rode towards them through the trees. It was too late to turn back now. Paul wouldn't let him off that easily.

"You actually came," Paul said, stopping his bike. "I didn't think you would. Does your friend want to ride, too?"

"Oh, no," Stephen said, shaking his head. "I'm just here to watch."

"Suit yourself," Paul said. He nodded to Jason. "Let's see what you can do."

Probably a whole lot of nothing, Jason thought. He shrugged. Then he and Stephen followed Paul down to the track.

* * *

Jason wanted to pretend the BMX track wasn't a big deal, but deep down he was impressed. There was a large clearing in the trees where a track had been created. Huge bumps and jumps were built into it.

They watched as one of Paul's friends hit the dirt ramp on the track and went airborne. The rider did a kick-out, pushing the left side of his bike out and back in, before landing back on the track.

"Not bad," Jason said. He tried to sound unimpressed. Stephen shook his head.

"Think you can do that?" Paul asked. On the track, another rider jumped. The second biker caught even bigger air than the first. He took both feet off the pedals in mid-air and kicked them wide. The rider brought his feet back to the pedals just before landing and cycling away.

"Not with this bike I can't," Jason said. "But maybe with one of those baby bikes." He was hoping Paul had forgotten to bring him a bike to ride.

"I brought my old bike for you," Paul said. "As promised."

Great, Jason thought. *I'm stuck now – no way out.*

CHAPTER 4

HIT THE DIRT

Jason sat on Paul's old BMX bike at the top of the hill. He took a deep breath. All the other riders had stopped what they were doing. They all stood near a picnic table along the side of the track watching him.

It feels strange sitting on such a tiny bike, Jason thought. The scuffed pads Paul had let him borrow were different, too. *I probably look more like an armoured knight than a BMX rider*, he thought.

"Whenever you're ready," Paul called. "After what you said this afternoon, we're expecting big things! Don't let us down!"

Jason pulled the full-face helmet over his head. After a few tries, he was able to click the chinstrap into place to make it snug.

Here goes nothing, Jason thought. He cranked the pedal and launched himself down the giant dirt hill.

Air whistled inside his helmet. He squatted down, and as the dirt bike hit the end of the jump, he pulled up. But instead of flying over the jump, the bike did a tiny hop. Jason's tyres landed back on the dirt, and he wobbled a bit.

It was nothing like landing on hard, flat pavement. The loose soil and rocks seemed to want to knock Jason right off of the bike.

Jason gripped the handlebars and stood up on the pedals, pedalling harder to gain some speed. He tore around the first turn.

Suddenly, his back wheel skidded right. Afraid the bike would drop him, he jerked to the left and whipped around the bend. Jason smiled as the bike straightened out.

His smile faded when he saw the double jump ahead of him.

"Get ready to laugh at me again," Jason mumbled.

He pedalled hard going up the first slope. Pulling on his handlebars, Jason tried to get more air off the jump. The bike seat hit him in the bum and threw him off balance. He fell, crashing and sliding downhill.

Someone in the crowd yelled, "Nice!" Everyone laughed.

Jason lay on his back, white dots dancing in front of his eyes. "Now I know why they wear the space helmets," he muttered.

Jason closed his eyes for a moment and heard footsteps approach. When he opened his eyes, Paul was standing over him. He held out his hand to help Jason up. Jason was embarrassed, but he let Paul pull him up to his feet.

"Not so easy, is it?" Paul asked, looking smug. That was enough to make Jason open his mouth again.

"If I had time to practice, I'd be as good as you guys," Jason said. As soon as the words were out, he wished he hadn't said them. Stephen groaned. Jason looked over at his friend. Stephen was shaking his head. The look on Stephen's face told Jason he'd said too much. Again.

CHAPTER 5

DOUBLE DARE

Paul reached into his back pocket and pulled out a folded slip of paper. He held it out to Jason and smiled. "Prove it," he said.

Jason unfolded the paper. It showed a picture of a BMX biker and the words "12th ANNUAL DIRT CROSS." Underneath were the details on how to enter the contest.

"Let's see how good you can get in two weeks," Paul said. "I'll even let you borrow my gear and bike to make it fair."

Stephen grabbed the flyer from Jason's hand. "No way," he said. "You'd be racing against riders who've been riding BMX bikes since they were kids."

Jason looked at the track Paul and his friends had made. He hadn't even made it around once without wiping out. And he'd be picking dirt out of his teeth for days.

"I don't know, Paul," Jason began. "Maybe Stephen's right."

"I double dare you," Paul said. He folded his arms and glanced back at his friends. "All you have to do is take a place in the race. You said you could do it. Show us."

"Fine," Jason said. He could taste the track dust in his mouth. "See you at the Dirt Cross in two weeks."

* * *

The trip home was tense. Jason felt like an idiot. He had to walk both his bike and Paul's BMX bike back home.

"You realize what you've done, don't you?" Stephen asked after a while.

"I know, I know. I opened my big mouth again," Jason said.

"That's not all," Stephen said. "You wiped out in front of a few boys from school tonight. Next time it'll be in front of a huge crowd, though!"

"I can do it, Stephen," Jason said. He struggled to balance both bikes. "I just need you to help me."

"No way," Stephen said. "If you want to risk hurting yourself, you're on your own."

"Please," Jason said. "I don't even care if I win. I just want to prove I can finish."

Stephen stopped walking suddenly.

Jason had to quickly steer the bikes to avoid hitting his friend. "What are you doing?" he asked.

"I'll make you a deal," Stephen said. "If I help you, you have to make a promise."

"Okay," Jason said.

"Promise me this is the last stupid dare," Stephen said. "I'm serious, Jason. And stop being such a big mouth all the time."

"No problem," Jason said. "I can do that. No sweat."

The friends shook on it. Stephen groaned and then laughed a little.

"We've got a lot of work to do," Stephen said. He pointed at Jason. "And you've got dirt on your forehead."

CHAPTER 6

TOUGH TRAINING

On Saturday morning, Jason headed to Pine River National Park to meet Stephen. It felt strange riding Paul's BMX bike across town. His legs were much more tired than when he rode his mountain bike.

"Why aren't we practising at the track with Paul and his friends?" Jason asked.

He looked around the picnic tables, wooded areas and paved trails in the park. It didn't look like a BMX course at all.

"They'll make you nervous," Stephen said. "You need to get comfortable on that bike before you do anything else. You need to learn to go up and down hills."

"This park is totally flat," Jason said. "Maybe this isn't the best place."

"There are miles and miles of dirt trails along the river," Stephen said. "Dave used to ride them until he fell over."

Great, Jason thought. *Just the way I want to spend my Saturday.*

Stephen pulled an old notebook from his backpack. "I borrowed this from my brother," he said. "It's every racing trick he collected from his BMX days. He and his team would write down what they did to win. And they added lessons from when they lost."

"Like a BMX instruction book?" Jason asked. "That's really cool." Stephen threw the book to him. Jason flipped through the pages. There were sketches of racetracks, jumps and notes on nearly every page.

Crouch down low over your seat to minimize wind drag, Jason read to himself.

That makes sense, he thought. *Standing up too high probably just slows you down.*

"I'm not sure it'll help," Stephen admitted. "But it's better than nothing."

"Cool," Jason said. "Where do we start, Coach?"

"You ride until your legs hurt," Stephen said. "Then you ride a bit more. Follow me."

* * *

Stephen wasn't joking. Jason spent the entire day racing through the rough, muddy, overgrown trails. More than a few times, he wiped out.

"Get up!" Stephen called. He followed from a distance on his mountain bike. "The race isn't over just because you fall. It ends when you cross the finish line!"

"You've got to be kidding me," Jason muttered. There was mud caked into the sprocket and cranks of the bike. One of the back wheel pegs was buried in the ground.

Fantastic, Jason thought, wiping the mud away. *I'll probably end up ruining Paul's bike before I get a chance to race with it.*

Stephen skidded to a stop and hopped off the bike. He pulled the BMX notebook out of his backpack and opened it.

"David's notes say one of the biggest mistakes riders make is giving up," Stephen said. "Once they fall off, they act as though the race is over. The best thing to do is get back on quickly and ride like you're on fire."

"Fine," Jason said. He picked up the bike and got back on. Silently, he rode off.

"Wait for me, Jason!" Stephen called.

At one point, Jason hit a huge pothole, knocking himself off of his bike. He flew over the handlebars and hit the ground hard. He lay there stunned.

"Are you okay?" Stephen called. He stopped his mountain bike to help Jason.

"Yeah," Jason said, groaning. "I'll live."

"Good," Stephen said. "Then get back on the bike! You have more work to do."

CHAPTER 7

READY OR NOT

Jason trained non-stop for the next two weeks. He and Stephen spent every spare moment they had at the park. Jason practised hopping over the tops of hills and controlling his speed around the corners.

"Always keep pedalling," Stephen read from the BMX book. "Never coast."

"What if I get tired?" Jason asked.

"You can coast after the race is over," Stephen said.

"Does it say that? Really?" Jason asked. He hoped Stephen was joking.

Stephen leaned over to show him the entry. "It does say you could try braking a little around the corners," Stephen said. "It'll help give you some control."

"I'll try it," Jason said. He was suddenly anxious to get moving. "Let's ride."

The two friends took off down the trail again. Jason hit a rise in the path, and his bike was launched high off the ground.

"Did you see that, Stephen?" Jason shouted. "I caught some major air!"

Stephen nodded. "Yeah," he said. "But the book says that jumps might look cool, but you're slowing yourself down by jumping too high. Stay low on jumps. You're faster on the ground."

"Huh," Jason said. "I wonder if Paul and his BMX big shots know that."

"I guess we'll find out," Stephen said, closing the BMX notebook.

* * *

On the last day of training, Stephen was far behind Jason on the path.

"Wait up," Stephen called. "Are you trying to lose me?"

Jason shrugged and slowed down. "Isn't that the idea?" he asked.

"I think you're getting the hang of it," Stephen said, smiling. "You might finish the race tomorrow after all."

"I hope so," Jason said.

"It'll be different with other riders on the track," Stephen told him. "It won't be easy."

"I just don't want to look stupid out there," Jason said. "It'll be cool to show Paul how far I've come."

As they rode back towards the main park area, Jason realized something. *I'm actually excited about the race*, he thought. *Maybe after the Dirt Cross, I'll tell Paul he was right.*

"One last thing," Stephen said. He turned and rode towards a group of picnic tables. "And it's pretty important."

Stephen stopped near a bench and pulled out the BMX book. He flipped to the page he was looking for and nodded.

"What?" Jason asked. He felt like he'd already learned everything he could.

"You have to learn how to balance at the start gate and how to get the hole-shot," Stephen said.

"The what-shot?" Jason asked. He didn't like the sound of that.

Stephen laughed. "The hole-shot is what they call it when you're the first one out of the gate," he explained. "Great BMX riders can tell when the gate is going to drop. They're pedalling before it hits the ground."

Jason sighed. "Isn't it enough to just pedal really fast?" he asked.

"There's a little more to it than that," Stephen said. "Ride over to that wall."

Jason rode over to the brick wall along the side of the park with Stephen.

"Okay, now get as close to the wall as you can with your front tyre," Stephen said, reading from a page in the book. "Get close enough that the tyre is touching the wall. You'll need to do that at the starting gate."

Jason did as he was told, but he still didn't understand.

"Use the wall to keep your balance," Stephen continued reading. "If you get tight enough up against the wall, you can keep both feet on the pedals. That way, you'll have the strength of both legs right away when the gate drops."

Jason nodded. "And that's how I'll get this holy-shot," he said.

"Hole-shot," Stephen corrected him.

"Whatever," Jason muttered, trying to balance.

It was tricky at first, but after a few tries, he mastered it. He knew it'd be different with other riders around, but at least he'd sort of look like he knew what to do.

Sort of.

CHAPTER 8
DIRT CROSS

"You have to be joking," Jason said as he stepped into the outdoor arena of the 12th Annual Dirt Cross on Saturday morning. He couldn't believe how many people were there. The stands were packed with spectators.

"I told you," Stephen said. "You don't want to back out, do you?"

"No way," Jason said. "I didn't spend the past two weeks in training for nothing."

He wheeled Paul's BMX bike to the check-in table and lined up. Jason watched the other riders pin their racing numbers to their shirts. Suddenly, he felt out of place.

Jason glanced around at the other riders at the registration table. Some of them were wearing shirts with logos on them.

"Why do their shirts have bike names on them?" Jason asked Stephen.

"They're probably sponsored or on a racing team like Dave was," Stephen said.

I didn't know I'd be racing the pros, Jason thought. He'd hoped his race would have at least a few people who raced for fun. "Last place, here I come," he muttered quietly.

After Jason filled out some forms, the woman at the desk handed him his racing number. Number 13.

"Oh, man," Jason said, groaning. "This can't be good."

"Lucky 13," Stephen said, smiling. He watched Jason pin the number to his sweatshirt. "Perfect!"

The under-10s race was just ending when Jason and Stephen walked over to the course.

"Looks like you're racing next," Stephen said. He slapped his friend on the back. "Are you ready?"

Jason nodded. "I think so," he said. "Any last tips from Dave's notebook?"

"Yeah," Stephen said. "Pedal fast. Really fast."

Great tip, Jason thought.

* * *

At the starting gate, Jason pulled on his helmet. Someone gave him a light shove from behind. When he turned around, he saw it was Paul.

"You actually turned up!" Paul said. "I'm impressed."

"Don't be too impressed yet," Jason said. He tightened his chinstrap. "You might not get your bike back in one piece."

"Tell you what," Paul said. "If you beat me, you can keep the bike."

Jason looked at the little bike Paul had let him use. It wasn't especially fancy like some of the others lined up next to him. Even so, Jason had learned a lot on it.

"Deal," Jason said. They shook on it.

"Riders, line up," a voice said over the loudspeaker.

Jason edged his front tyre so that it was pressed against the gate and stood up on both pedals. He was ready to surge ahead as soon as the gate fell.

As the last of the riders took their places, Jason had a terrible thought. What if Paul tried to mess with him on purpose?

He bet his bike on this, Jason thought. *He'll want to make sure he wins.*

Jason took a deep breath and looked over the twisting stretch of track. A horn sounded. The gate dropped.

The race was on!

CHAPTER 9
MUD SANDWICH

It took Jason a second to realize the gate had dropped. By the time he started pedalling, most of the riders were off.

So much for that hole-shot, Jason thought. *I'm already behind.*

Jason heard Stephen shout, "Let's go, Jason!" Jason's tyres rolled over the metal gate and picked up speed on the first hill. He held the grips tightly as he raced to the first jump.

Jason heard the other bikers hit the jump next to him. Then he was in the air. He stiffened up and prepared to land. Then he remembered what Dave had written.

Make your body like a set of shocks. Don't tense up!

Jason relaxed a bit as the tyres hit the dirt. He wobbled but kept his balance.

So far so good, Jason thought. He crouched low and pedalled hard as he raced towards the next stretch of rollers.

As he hit the first bump, Jason leaned back and pulled a manual. He popped his front wheel up and stopped pedalling.

Bringing his front wheel back to the ground, he cranked the pedals with his legs and continued over the course. He sped over the bumps like he was on flat ground.

Nice! Jason thought, setting his front wheel down. He barrelled into the first strip and rode the curve high and outside to pass three other riders. He could see the four leaders in front of him. Paul was trying to pass the rider in first place.

If I stay here, I'll end up in fifth, Jason thought. *But then I won't get to keep this bike!*

With a surge of speed, Jason pedalled hard. He kept his eyes on the upcoming tabletop. He hit the ramp at the same time as another rider. Even so, Jason kept his jump low, just like the BMX book had said.

Jason leaned forward to cut through the wind and landed clean on the other side. The other rider wasn't so lucky. He wiped out and flew over the top of his handlebars. Jason didn't dare look back. He blazed along the track, heading into the next turn.

He was getting close to the end, so Jason pumped the pedals with everything he had. He was gaining on the other riders. He hit the next series of rollers. *Bam! Bam! Bam!* In moments, he was right behind Paul and the other three leaders.

As they moved towards the last strip, the rider in second place twisted his handlebars too far to the left. His bike hit Paul's. The blow was hard enough to knock him off of his bike. As Paul fell, his bike veered into the second-place rider.

Before Jason knew it, all four of the leaders had crashed into the bank of the track. He tried to steer away from the wreckage, but he couldn't. His tyre rammed into the pile of fallen bikes, and Jason found himself on top of the heap of riders.

CHAPTER 10

THE BIG FINISH

Get up! Jason thought. He could almost hear Stephen's voice. It's what he'd said everytime Jason fell during training. Thanks to those falls, Jason was good at getting back on his bike. As the others tried to untangle their bikes, Jason was already up.

The crowd cheered as Jason grabbed his bike. The pedals and chain were full of mud, but it didn't matter. No one would wait for him to clean off his bike.

He remembered what the BMX book said: *Get back on and ride like you're on fire!*

Jason swung his leg over the seat and jammed his foot onto the pedal. He cranked hard and rode away from the crash. Jason heard the other riders shout after him as they climbed onto their bikes.

Jason tore along the track. The rush of racing was unlike anything he'd ever felt. He hit the hip jumps, remembering to stay low, and landed clean. He didn't bother trying any fancy moves. The race wasn't about showing off. It was about finishing.

Jason rode high going into the last turn and cut in to gain more speed. He coasted and did a manual over three short rollers. Behind him, the riders grunted as they pedalled as hard as they could.

Then Paul shouted at him, "Take it, Tillman! Win this thing!"

Does he actually want me to win the race? Jason thought, surprised.

The other riders were getting closer. Jason's legs burned from pedalling so hard. The wind whistled through his helmet, and his fingers tightened on the grips.

Jason looked up and saw the finish line just ahead. He glanced over his shoulder. Another rider was just behind him, fighting to catch up. Paul was in third.

With a final burst of speed, Jason surged forward. The crowd cheered as Jason tore across the finish line.

First place!

"Yes!" Jason shouted. He raised his arms in victory.

CHAPTER 11

A GOOD SPORT

"I can't believe it," Stephen shouted as he ran over to where Jason and Paul were standing.

Paul smiled at Jason. "You tore it up out there," Paul said. "Congratulations."

"Thanks, man," Jason said. "But I can't take your bike."

"It's yours," Paul said. "A deal is a deal. Besides, you'll need that bike for next time."

"Thanks, Paul," Jason said. "You know, I was wrong about BMX racing. It's a lot harder than it looks. I had fun, though!"

"Keep at it," Paul said. "You were born to ride a baby bike."

Jason laughed. *Paul isn't so bad after all,* he thought.

"Thanks," Jason said.

Paul hopped back on his bike and rode off towards his friends. "See you at the track sometime, Tillman," Paul called over his shoulder.

"I'm still amazed," Stephen said, shaking his head. "First place. I didn't think you'd even finish."

"I got lucky," Jason said. Then he frowned. "Hey, wait a second. You didn't think I'd finish?"

Just then, a man in a Mudd Ripper Bikes jacket appeared. He smiled at Jason and held out his hand.

"Otto Jones," he said. "I represent the Mudd Ripper racing team."

"Hi," Jason said, shaking Mr. Jones's hand. "I'm Jason Tillman."

"That was one of the best races I've seen in a long time," Mr Jones said. "You really kept it together after that crash."

"Thanks," Jason said.

"We're looking to fill a few spots on our team this summer," Mr. Jones continued. "Are you interested in racing for us at the weekends?"

Jason blinked and nodded. He couldn't believe what he was hearing. For once he was speechless.

Mr Jones handed Jason a business card. "Give me a call after you've talked to your parents," he said. "We could really do with someone like you on the team." With that, he turned and headed towards the car park.

"Wow," Stephen said. "The one time you could open your mouth, you keep quiet!"

Jason stared at the card. He thought about what Mr Jones had said.

We're looking to fill a few spots.

"I'll be right back," Jason told Stephen.

Jason zipped through the fans, ducked under a rope barrier and slipped between two cars in the car park. He spotted Mr Jones just as he opened the door to his car.

"Mr Jones! Wait a second," Jason called. He braked to a stop next to Mr Jones's car.

Mr Jones seemed surprised, but smiled kindly. "What's up, Jason?" he asked.

"First of all, I'd love to join the team. I'll see what my parents say," Jason said.

"Excellent," Mr Jones replied.

"You said you needed to fill a few spots on the team, right?" Jason asked. "You should add my friend Paul, too. He's the one who got me into BMX biking."

Mr Jones frowned. "Was he here today?" he asked.

"Paul took third place," Jason said. "He probably would've won if he hadn't been knocked over."

"He showed promise too," Mr Jones said. He nodded. "Ask him to call me. We'll give him a shot."

ABOUT THE AUTHOR

Thomas Kingsley Troupe writes, makes movies and works as a firefighter. He's written many books for children, including *Ghostly Goalie* and *Phantom's Favourite*, and has two sons of his own. He likes zombies, bacon, orange ice lollies and reading stories to his children. Thomas currently lives in Minnesota, USA, with his family.

ABOUT THE ILLUSTRATOR

When Sean Tiffany was growing up, he lived on a small island off the coast of Maine, USA. Every day until he graduated from high school, he had to take a boat to get to school! Sean has a pet cactus called Jim.

Jason shook Mr Jones's hand again. Then he watched the man climb into his car and drive away. A moment later, Stephen ran over.

"They're handing out the trophies soon," Stephen said. "What are you doing?"

"Nothing," Jason said. "Just returning a favour. I'm using my big mouth to do something good for once."

"About time!" Stephen said, laughing.

Jason turned to his best friend and put an arm around his shoulder. They walked back towards the stands together.

"You know, Stephen," Jason said. "If I'm on the Mudd Ripper BMX team, I'm going to need a coach ..."

GLOSSARY

astronaut someone who travels in space

barrier bar, fence or wall that prevents something from going past it

cluster group of the same thing growing closely together

crank handle that is attached at a right angle to a shaft and turned to make a machine work

minimize make something as small as possible

soil dirt or earth

sprocket wheel with a rim made of tooth-like points that fit into the holes of a chain; the chain then drives the wheel

tense nervous or worried

track prepared path or course

DISCUSSION QUESTIONS

1. Did Jason do the right thing when he accepted Paul's dare? Why or why not?

2. Why does Jason get into so much trouble with dares? Can you list other ways he could deal with dares in the future?

3. At first, Jason doesn't think he'll like BMX riding. Talk about something you enjoy that at first you didn't think you would.

WRITING PROMPTS

1. Write about a time that you accepted a
dare you wish you hadn't. What was the
dare? What were the consequences?

2. Has a friend ever helped you learn
something new? Have you ever helped a
friend? Write about it.

3. What do you think happens after this
story ends? Write a chapter that tells the
reader what happens next.

MORE ABOUT BMX

BMX is a cycling sport made up of extreme, motocross-style racing on tracks with incline starts and obstacles all over the course. The sport allows riders to have a lot of personal creativity. BMX stands for two things: bicycle motocross racing (the "x" stands for "cross") and the style of bike itself. Here's how BMX got its start:

EARLY 1970s – BMX begins with children in southern California riding on dirt tracks and concrete skate parks. These early riders were imitating their motocross heroes, who rode bikes with engines.

1972 – The motorcycle racing documentary *On Any Sunday* is released and inspires a national BMX movement in the United States.

MID 1970s – BMX gains popularity and manufacturers start making bikes designed specifically for the sport.

1977 – The American Bicycle Association (ABA) is founded as the governing group for BMX in the United States.

1981 – The International BMX Federation is founded.

1982 – The first world championships for BMX are held a year later.

2003 – International Olympic Committee makes BMX a full-medal Olympic sport.

2008 – BMX is included in the Summer Olympic Games in Beijing, China. Maris Štrombergs, from Latvia, and Anne-Caroline Chausson, from France, are crowned the first Olympic champions.

Today, freestyle BMX is one of the major events at the Summer X Games. The popularity of freestyle BMX keeps growing, thanks to the availability of places to ride and do tricks.